MEGA MASH-UP

Robots vs. Gorillas in the Desert

Nikalas Catlow
Tim Wesson

Draw your own adventure!

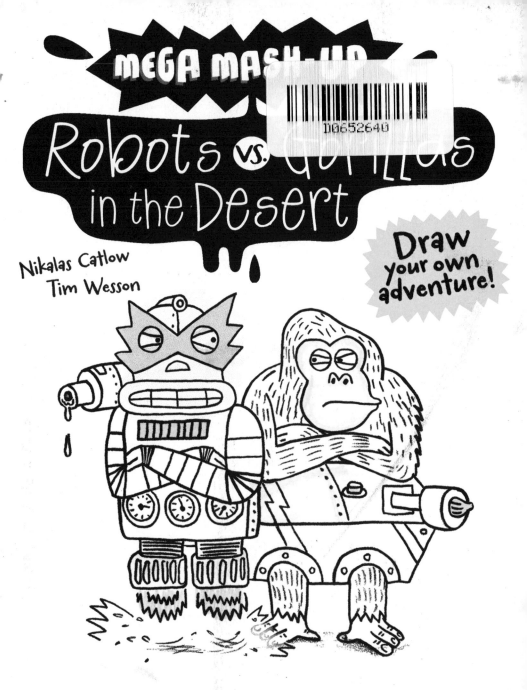

D0652640

nosy crow

An imprint of Candlewick Press

An imprint of Candlewick Press

Copyright © 2011 by Nikalas Catlow and Tim Wesson

All rights reserved. No part of this book may be reproduced, transmitted, or stored in an information retrieval system in any form or by any means, graphic, electronic, or mechanical, including photocopying, taping, and recording, without prior written permission from the publisher.

First U.S. edition 2011

Library of Congress Cataloging-in-Publication Data is available.

Library of Congress Catalog Card Number pending

ISBN 978-0-7636-5873-1

11 12 13 14 15 16 BVG 10 9 8 7 6 5 4 3 2 1

Printed in Berryville, VA, U.S.A.

This book was typeset in Agenda.
The illustrations were created digitally.

Nosy Crow
an imprint of
Candlewick Press
99 Dover Street
Somerville, Massachusetts 02144

www.nosycrow.com
www.candlewick.com

Your hand

This book needs

YOU!

What if ROBOTS and GORILLAS had a race in the **DESERT?** What if they got **SLIMED** by stinky SAND SLUGS on the way and had to grapple with famous WRESTLING SCORPIONS?

Who would win this **wacky race?**

You'll have to finish the illustrations and find out. . . .

Prepare to **LAUGH** while you doodle and SNICKER while you read.

INTRODUCING the Robots from Nanaville

Mega-Bite

Robotron

Gadget the Great

iBot

Multi-Tool

Introducing the Gorillas from Jungoil

Silverback Steve

Ape-Face

King Well-Hairy

Nobby Knuckles

Grappling Sam

You'll need these. . . .

DRAWING tools

These are the **3** tools that Nikalas and Tim used to create the artwork in this book.

PEN

crayon

felt-tip pen or marker

pencil

crayon

Using different tools helps create great drawings.

texture page

pen zigzags

crayon rubbing from linoleum floor

pencil cross-hatching

crayon rubbing from wood floor

pencil rubbing from wooden door

scribbly pencil

There are lots of ways you can add texture to your artwork. Here are a few examples.

crayon rubbing from wall

pencil dashes

pen circles

DRAWING TIP!
Turn to the back of the book for ideas on stuff you might want to draw in this adventure.

Chapter 1
Yes,
We Have
No
Bananas

The **Robots** zoom around a high-tech banana plantation called **Nanaville**. The two civilizations trade bananas and oil. Everyone is happy — for now. . . .

Add more banana trees.

Finish the stunned crowd.

One day, the two leaders meet. "Hello," says **King Well-Hairy**, crushing **Gadget the Great** to his huge gorilla chest in greeting. "**Hel-p!**" cries Gadget the Great, **Shocked**. Sparks shoot out of his head, sending **10,000 volts** of electricity up King Well-Hairy's nose.

"You fried my nose," sputters King Well-Hairy. "We're not giving you any more oil."

"You made me short-circuit," **bleeps** Gadget the Great. "You can't have any more bananas."

Five minutes later, **HUNGRY** and **SQUEAKY**, they decide to settle their differences with a race through the **Desert of Doom** instead.

"If the Gorillas win—and we will—we get all the bananas," declares King Well-Hairy.

Start

Draw an oasis.

Add skulls.

"If the Robots win—and we will—we get all the oil," responds Gadget the Great.

But no one realizes that there's no finish line! This is going to be a **VERY LONG RACE!**

This map needs lots more sand dunes and desert stuff.

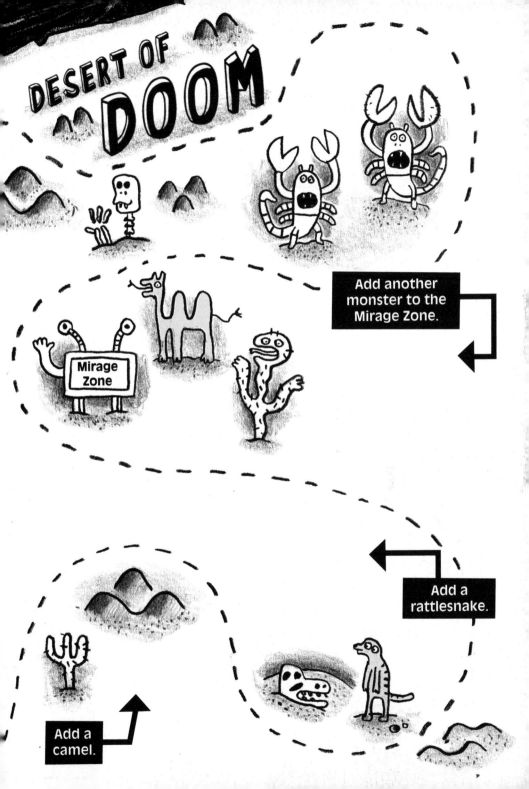

The Robots are preparing for the race. "Let's use our cool **OiL-fiRiNg bazookas** on those dumb Gorillas!" says Robotron with a chortle. "I can't wait to see them fall on their hairy bottoms!"

Finish iBot's oil bazooka.

Give Nanobot a heat-seeking oil bazooka.

Add texture and color to the sand.

Meanwhile the Gorillas are loading their **banana-firing tank suits** with ammo. "Those stupid Robots won't know what hit 'em!" hoots Grappling Sam.

But the **Desert of Doom** isn't called the **Desert of Doom** for nothing. . . .

Chapter 2
Start Yer Engines

Gorillas and Robots jostle one another at the starting dune. "**Get lost, Rusty!**" cries Nobby Knuckles. "**Eat boogers, banana breath!**" shouts Bitomatic. And they're off!

Nine hundred and ninety-nine years and six months, 15 days, 3 hours, 36 minutes, and 48 seconds later, the race is **Still going on**.

What is Nobby Knuckles day-dreaming about?

"I want a yummy banana!" complains Nobby Knuckles. "You can't have any. **THEY'RE OUR AMMUNITION!**" snaps Grappling Sam.

Meanwhile the Robots are so thirsty, they've started making **terrible clanking noises**. "I'm seizing up," cries Mega-Bite. "My nuts and bolts are shriveling."

Ooooooh! That doesn't sound good.

CREAK

Add some great clanking noises.

It's time for some dirty tactics. "Help me turn this sign around," says Grappling Sam, chuckling hairily. "We'll send those rusty robots in completely the wrong direction and into this trap!"

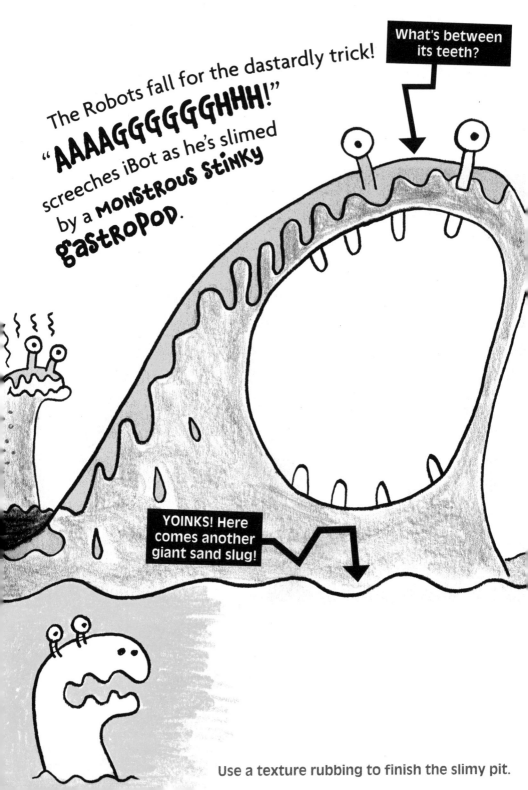

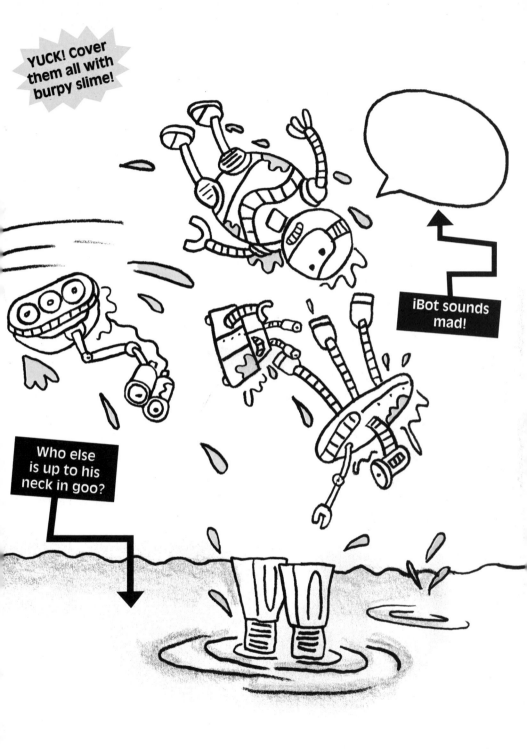

The Robots slither slimily out of the sand slugs' **Stinky Pit**, to find they've overtaken the Gorillas! "It must've been a shortcut!" cheers Mega-Bite.

Who is this giant garlic-burp-breath sand slug chasing?

Give this banana bar a fancy name!

Finish the woody texture.

What's going on in the window?

Throw down a couple of banana peels!

"Revenge will be ours!" exclaims iBot. They build a fake banana bar — on **QUICKSAND!** "Those stupid Gorillas'll do anything for a banana-mocha-cappuccino!"

"Oooh, oooh, oooh, make mine a large — aaahhh!" hollers Nobby Knuckles as he tumbles into the quicksand. The other Gorillas all pile in, and soon **tHeY aRe SiNkiNg fast**. . . .

Give the walls a woody texture.

OH, NO! Fill the pit with sinking Gorillas!

The Gorillas haul themselves out of the quicksand and drag their knuckles on toward the **oasis checkpoint**.

Chapter 3
The Megawatt -BOT Plot

"I can't see any of those **walking trash cans**. We must be in the lead!" cheers Ape-Face.

"Oooh! Look at that delicious bunch of bananas!" exclaims Nobby.

But suddenly a trap hidden by palm leaves flips up over his head. The Gorillas are caught!

OASIS THIS WAY

It's not a trick, honest!

Who's hiding behind here?

Draw more Gorillas in the trap.

Add texture to the rock.

"Mwa ha ha!" laugh the Robots, clanking out of hiding. "Now you will help us win the race, you overgrown monkeys. Who cares if we're seizing up? When you start running, your hairy legs will power our Megawatt-BOT and **victory will be ours!**"

What else is hiding in the palm trees?

Add leafy texture.

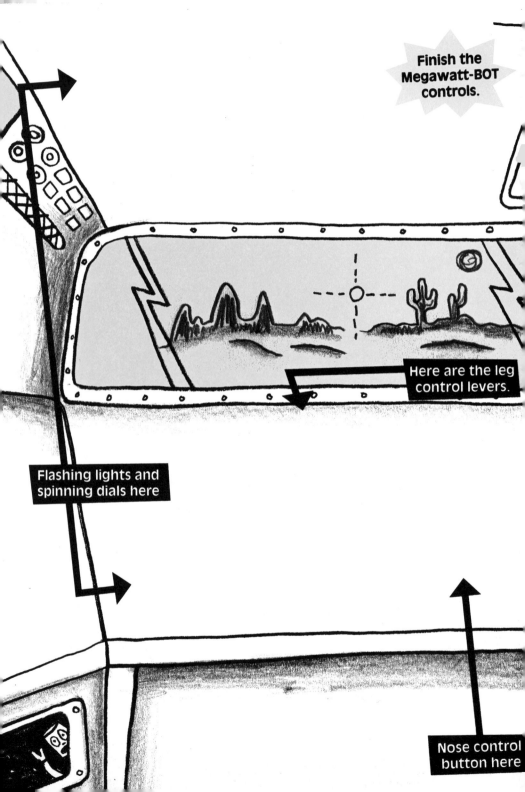

Multi-Tool starts fiddling with
the Megawatt-BOT's control panel.
"The resonating polarizing regulators
and gravitational particle beam
are ready!" he says.

"Show-off," mutters Nobby Knuckles.

"Setting the charge to **6,000 VOLTS!**"
cries Robotron.

Add another
robotic arm.

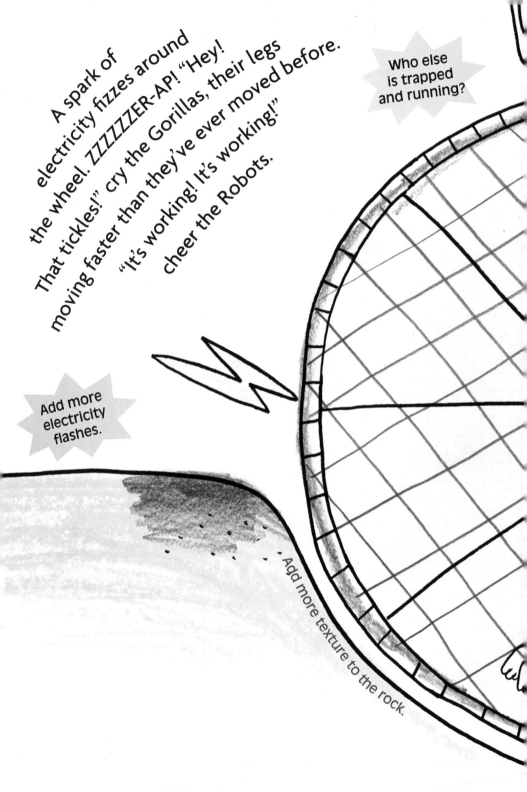

Add more palm leaves.

The **Megawatt-BOT** spins off into the desert, plowing through the cactus forest and flattening everything in its way! The Robots are still cheering as they leave a path of devastation behind them. . . .

Finish the cactus forest. Who else has gotten stuck?

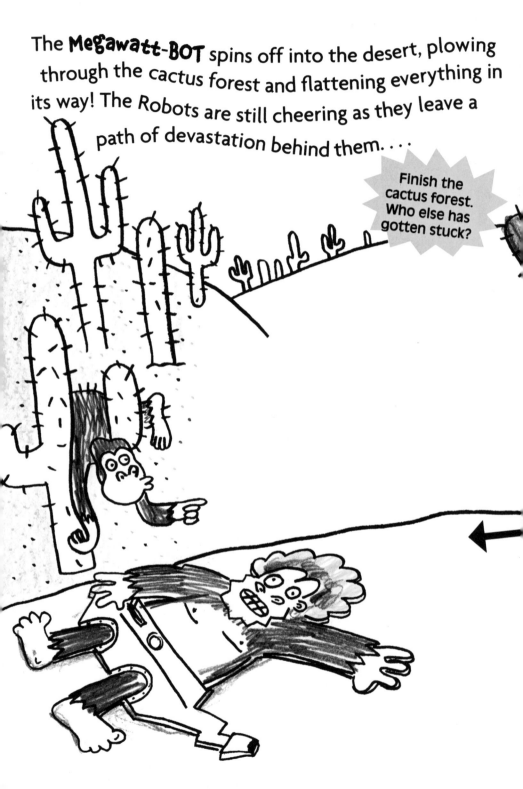

But seconds later, **CLATTER**, **CRUNCH**, the Megawatt-BOT plows into a stinky old camel pit, **DISINTEGRATING** into pieces!

What else is exploding out of the Megawatt-BOT crash?

Add a broken resonating polarizing regulator.

Chapter 4
Do you See what I See?

Grappling Sam and Nobby Knuckles are flung from the wheel into the lead. "Look at that massive **banana ice cream!**" cries Nobby, pointing greedily. "Hmmm," says Sam. "There's something funny about that banana. . . ."

Yikes! Add more flying debris.

Draw a vulture circling overhead.

The fierce desert heat starts to play more tricks on the gullible Gorillas.

"**MONSTERS, MONSTERS** everywhere!" cries Nobby, diving out of sight.

"What monsters?" asks Grappling Sam.

Sam thinks he's wrestling with his old enemy, the Hairminator. Except he's not. "Oooh, oooh, oooh, you're going down," he chants. "**AAAAGGHHHH!!**" screams Sam, in needle-sharp pain.

Sam thinks a cactus looks like the Hairminator.

Nobby Knuckles rubs **SAND FROM HIS eyes.**
"I keep thinking I can see Robots!" he says to Sam.
"CURSE THESE WRETCHED MIRAGES!"
"Those ARE Robots," points out Sam, pulling cactus
needles out of his face. "They've caught up with us.
OUCH!"

Sounds painful!

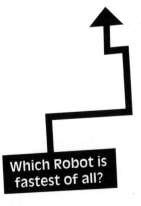

Leaving the Mirage Zone behind them, they all race on toward **SCORPION TOWN**. "Could this be a place where giant scorpions meet and fight to the death, just for fun?" wonders Grappling Sam. They'll soon find out. . . .

What do they look like?

Finish the notice board.

SCORPION

WRESTLING
KING STING VS. CLENCHER CLAW

SCORPION TOWN

what else is stuck to the cactus?

Chapter 5
Get Ready for Some Stinging Clenches!

Firing off bananas and oil at each other, the racers enter Scorpion Town. "**Take that, banana breath!**" Robotron cries as a stream of oil splats on to Grappling Sam's head. **Greasy!**

But someone is watching them. . . .

Suddenly, two giant scorpions in full wrestling gear appe
"I am King Sting!" says the first. "My killer specialty
is the deadly tail swipe!" SWOOSH, SWOOSH!

"I am Clencher Claw!" says the other. "My killer specialty is a vise-like grip and squish!" SNAP, SNAP!

WOWEE! What does Clencher Claw look like?

The racers are shocked. "Quick! Let's run away!" says Bitomatic. But Grappling Sam likes to wrestle. "**No, Let's fight!**" he says. What will they do?

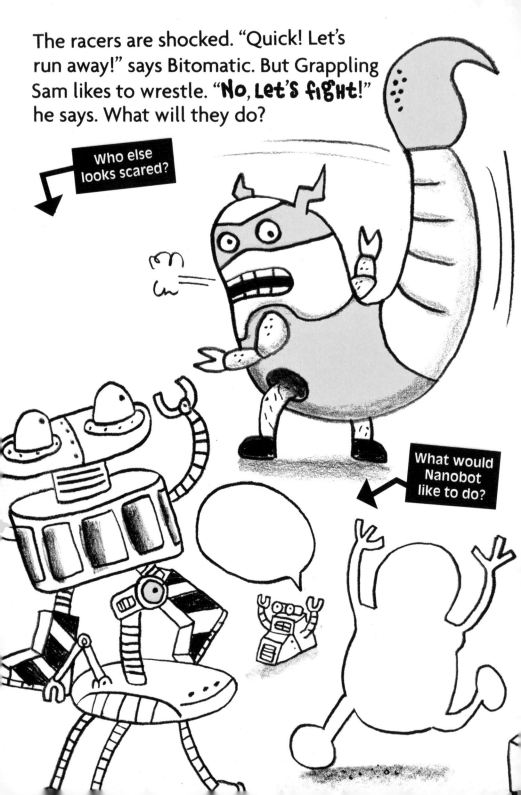

Who else looks scared?

What would Nanobot like to do?

Everyone is fighting everyone!

It's not looking good for the Gorillas. But then Grappling Sam pulls his old wrestling move, The Hook, on King Sting. **THE SCORPION GOES DOWN!** But Clencher Claw is still going strong. . . .

"Let's use our **secret weapon**!" declares Robotron.
"Activate the **LOONY LASER beam**, Robots!"

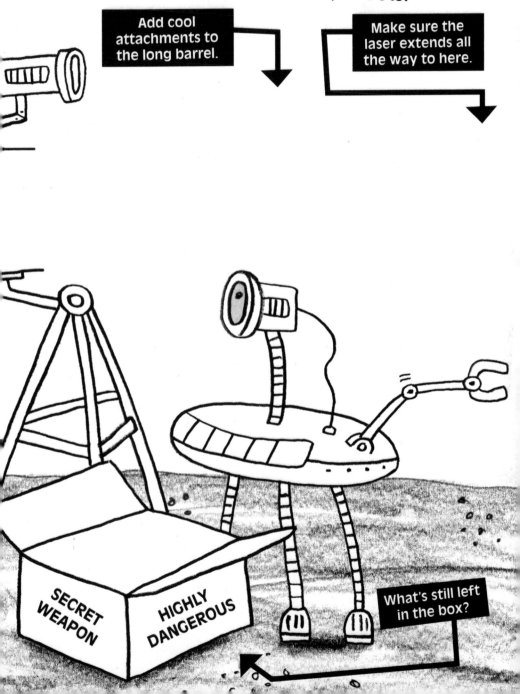

Add cool attachments to the long barrel.

Make sure the laser extends all the way to here.

SECRET WEAPON

HIGHLY DANGEROUS

What's still left in the box?

The Gorillas stagger around dizzily.
"I'm all singed," sniffs Ape-Face.

Add some dazed Robots.

The Robots buzz around, looking worse for the wear. "**My SPROCKETS ARE SMOKING**," puffs Robotron.

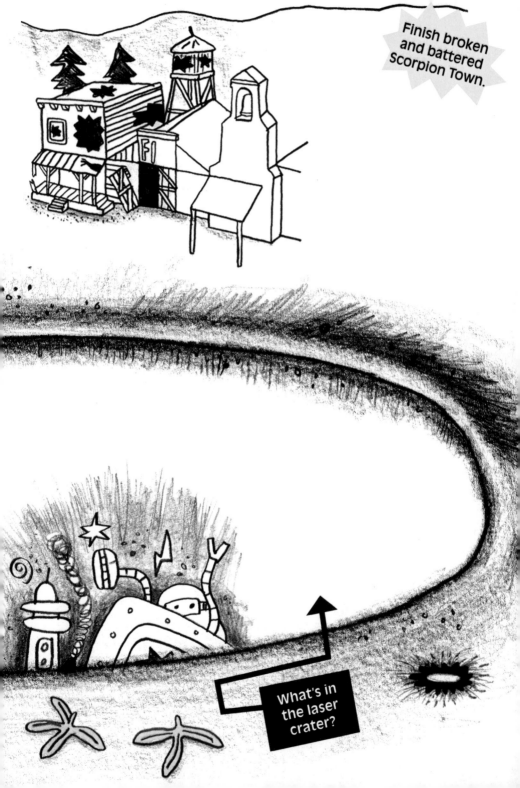

All that's left of the nastiest wrestling giant scorpions in the world are two pairs of **SMOLDERING PANTS**. But the race must go on!

Chapter 6
Here We Go Again

Hungry and squeaky, the Gorillas and Robots arrive at a familiar place. **"WE'RE AT THE STARTING DUNE AGAIN,"** protests Sam. "I think we've been going around in circles," adds a dizzy Multi-Tool.

Boy, does he look angry!

Everyone looks puzzled.

The Gorillas and Robots decide to call the race a draw. "**Mmmmmm** ... **bananas** ..." murmurs Nobby Knuckles as the Gorillas celebrate with an **all-you-can-eat Bananathon**.

Who's peeking over the table?

Add a giant banana sundae.

Create a mega mash-up banana feast!

BACK IN NANAVILLE, the Robots are filling a swimming pool with oil. Robotron slips and falls headfirst into the pool. "That's good stuff," he says with a laugh. "**I'M WELL OILED NOW!**"

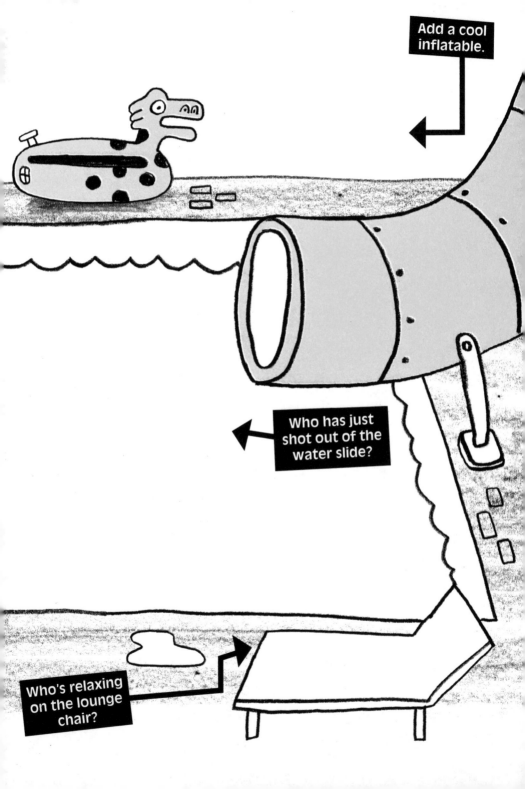

"**OOOH! OOOH! OOOH!**" cry the Gorillas as Grappling Sam and Nobby Knuckles pass by on their **spectacular banana float**.

Litter the ground with banana peels.

The two Gorillas fling bananas into the cheering crowd.

Finish the cheering Gorilla crowd!

During the closing ceremony there is a signing of **the great treaty** between King Well-Hairy and Gadget the Great. "Hello," says King Well-Hairy, **CRUSHING** Gadget the Great to his huge gorilla chest in greeting. **"HeL-P!"** cries Gadget the Great, **SHOCKED**.

Add zapping sound effects.

Finish the shocked leaders!

Sparks shoot out of Gadget's head, sending 10,000 volts of electricity up King Well-Hairy's nose. The two leaders lie **fizzling in the dust**.

How is the crowd reacting?

Picture Glossary

If you get stuck or need ideas, then use these pages for reference.

If you like, you can copy the pictures. OR you can draw your own versions.

OIL-FIRING BAZOOKAS

Smart 3000

Deluxe XLZ10

TREE HOUSES

Multi-story

Single-story

SHERRIF'S OFFICE

OIL DRIP

OIL TANKER

OIL SPLAT

Ha Ha

HOOT!

SPLAT

WHACK

SOUND EFFECTS

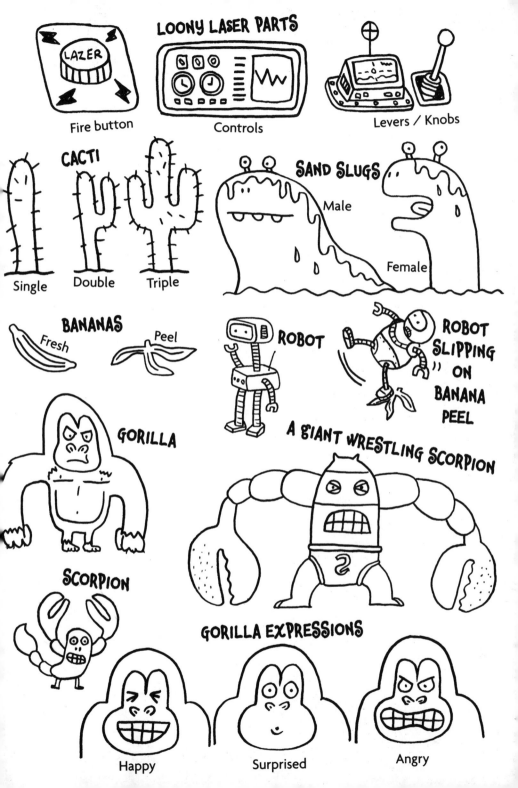

Visit our **awesome** website and get involved!

www.megamash-up.com
Upload artwork and get the latest news